TIME TWISTERS

ABIGAIL ADAMS

PIRATE of the CARIBBEAN

ALSO BY STEVE SHEINKIN

KING GEORGE: WHAT WAS HIS PROBLEM?

TWO MISERABLE PRESIDENTS

WHICH WAY TO THE WILD WEST?

THE NOTORIOUS BENEDICT ARNOLD: A TRUE
STORY OF ADVENTURE, HEROISM & TREACHERY

BOMB: THE RACE TO BUILD—AND STEAL—THE
WORLD'S MOST DANGEROUS WEAPON

THE PORT CHICAGO 50: DISASTER, MUTINY,
AND THE FIGHT FOR CIVIL RIGHTS

MOST DANGEROUS: DANIEL ELLSBERG AND THE
SECRET HISTORY OF THE VIETNAM WAR

UNDEFEATED: JIM THORPE AND THE CARLISLE
INDIAN SCHOOL FOOTBALL TEAM

TIME TWISTERS: ABRAHAM LINCOLN,
PRO WRESTLER

TIME TWISTERS

ABIGAIL ADAMS

PIRATE of the CARIBBEAN

STEVE SHEINKIN

ILLUSTRATED BY **NEIL SWAAB**

ROARING BROOK PRESS

New York

Published by Roaring Brook Press

Roaring Brook Press is a division of Holtzbrinck Publishing Holdings Limited Partnership

175 Fifth Avenue, New York, NY 10010

mackids.com

Library of Congress Control Number: 2017944498

ISBN: 978-1-250-14893-3

Our books may be purchased in bulk for promotional, educational, or business use. Please contact your local bookseller or the Macmillan Corporate and Premium Sales Department at (800) 221-7945 ext. 5442 or by e-mail at MacmillanSpecialMarkets@macmillan.com.

First edition 2018

Book design by Neil Swaab

Printed in the United States of America by LSC Coummunications, Harrisonburg, Virginia

1 3 5 7 9 10 8 6 4 2

For Braiden White's second-grade class at Division Street Elementary—thanks for all the great ideas!

CHAPTER ONE

"**T**his place is a disaster," Abigail Adams said. "Look at this."

She made her mouth into the shape of an O and puffed out a cloud of frosty fog.

"It *is* chilly in here," John Adams agreed, rubbing his hands together. "Not quite ready to be lived in, perhaps."

It was November 1800 in the new capital city of Washington. Abigail and John Adams were standing in a huge, empty room in the President's House—soon to be known as the White House. They had just moved in, but John was right. The house was far from ready.

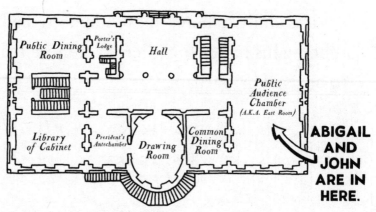

White House Plans
(First Floor)

ABIGAIL AND JOHN ARE IN HERE.

Only six of the thirty-six rooms were finished. The walls had wide gaps that still needed plaster. There was a second floor—but no staircase to it. Even with fires burning in every fireplace, the air inside was damp and bone-chilling.

2

John Adams pulled on his overcoat. "Well, I'd best be off," he said. "I'm meeting with Mr. Jefferson this afternoon. I'll leave you to your work."

"Hanging laundry," Abigail groaned. "Yet again."

"What's that, dear?"

"That's my work today, hanging wet clothes up to dry," she said.

"Oh, good," John said. "I'm out of clean stockings."

Wet pants and dresses hung from strings stretched across the room. It wasn't a great place to dry clothes, but the only other option was the yard, which was knee-deep mud.

Abigail snatched a shirt from a large laundry basket. "I hung laundry in the East Room of the White House." She tossed the shirt toward a string. It missed and landed on the floor. "That's what people know about me."

"Who are you talking to, dear?"

"You," she said. "The children reading this. Anyone who will listen."

John Adams turned toward the readers— he looked right at YOU.

he said.

Then he buttoned his coat.

"History books describe you as a brave patriot, a leader in Congress during the American Revolution." Abigail grabbed a pair of pants from the basket. "And now you're the second president of the United States. But what do they say about me? Cute little 'fun facts.' I was the first First Lady to live in the White House. And I hung laundry to dry in the East Room. As if women can do nothing better than wash clothing! How very amusing!"

She threw the pants over her shoulder. They landed on her husband's head.

SPLAT!

"Well, um . . ." John said, pulling the wet pants from his face. "I shouldn't keep the vice president waiting."

"If I have to hang laundry one more time, I am going to scream!" Abigail said, sort of screaming. "Did you know there were women pirates?"

"Pirates? Where?" John said, looking around.

"Back in the early 1700s, in what's called the Golden Age of pirates in the Caribbean. Some of the most famous pirates were women. Anne Bonny, Mary Read . . ."

"Dear, what are you telling me? That you wish to become a pirate?"

"I'm telling you women can do *anything*," Abigail said. "I've been trying to tell you for *years*. I suppose I shall have to prove it to you. I won't be gone long. Give my regards to Mr. Jefferson."

President Adams seemed confused. Also a bit worried.

But he left for his meeting.

Abigail Adams stood alone in the East

Room, staring at the laundry basket.

"I wonder if it would really work?" she said. "Only one way to find out."

She ran across the room, jumped, and sailed into the basket.

And she was gone.

CHAPTER TWO

"**O**kay guys, it's that time again," Ms. Maybee told her fourth-grade class. "That moment you lie awake at night dreaming about! Yes, you guessed it—it's time to get out your history textbooks!"

Most of the kids groaned.

"Don't give me that," Ms. Maybee said, laughing. "You thought Abraham Lincoln was going to be boring, right? And look how much fun he turned out to be!"

That was true. The class did like Abe Lincoln.

"Well, today we meet another great American," Ms. Maybee told the class. "One of my personal favorites: Abigail Adams!"

I've heard of her!

Doc said.

DOC.
(HE BROKE HISTORY.)

Kids looked at Doc, stunned. He used to complain louder than anyone when it was time to learn history.

9

"Good for you, Doc," said Ms. Maybee. "And what can you tell us about her? What is Abigail Adams famous for?"

Doc looked to Abby, his stepsister, hoping for help.

She shrugged.

"I could tell you," Doc said. "But won't it be more fun if we all learn together?"

ABBY.
(SHE ALSO BROKE HISTORY.)

Ms. Maybee smiled. "In other words, you have no idea."

"Not a clue," Doc said.

"We'll learn together then," Ms. Maybee said, pointing to the textbook on Doc's desk. "Page sixty-five, right at the top."

All the kids opened their books to page sixty-five. The heading said:

Abigail Adams in the White House

There was a painting of the city of Washington in the early 1800s. The White House was there, but not much else—just fields and trees.

Doc began to read aloud:

In 1800, our nation's capital was still under construction.

Washington, DC, had wide dirt streets, but few finished buildings.

One of the construction sites was the President's House, which later became known as the White House.

President John Adams and his wife, Abigail Adams, were the first to live in this new building.

But Abigail Adams was no longer there.

She had disappeared that morning and not returned.

She had said something about wanting to be a pirate.

"Very funny," Ms. Maybee said. "Only, please note that I'm not actually laughing."

"What'd I do?" Doc asked.

"Just read what the book says."

"I am," Doc said.

"He *is*," Abby said.

Other kids nodded. All their books said the same thing.

Ms. Maybee checked her copy of the book. "Huh, you're right. I'm sorry, Doc, please continue."

Doc read:

John Adams was worried. He did not want his wife to become a pirate.

In addition, he was all out of clean stockings.

He spent the afternoon hanging wet clothes up to dry in the East Room, and watching out the window for his wife.

But Abigail Adams did not come home.

"Keep reading, Doc!" someone called from the back of the room.

Doc turned to the next page. "That's all it says about her."

"Where'd she go?" another kid asked.

"Did she become a pirate?"

"I don't know," Ms. Maybee said. "I mean, I'm glad you're all so excited about history. But I have to tell you, I don't remember this story at all."

Because this story had never happened before. It's not how history was supposed to go.

Doc and Abby looked at each other. "Oh, no," Abby whispered.

CHAPTER THREE

About three years before this story takes place, Abby's mom had married Doc's dad. And everyone got along, mostly. That was the good part. The bad part was that both parents worked late. Abby's mom (by now Doc called her "mom" too) was a teacher at their school and ran an after-school program for younger kids. Their dad taught at the middle school and stayed late to coach track. So every day, after school, Abby and Doc had to stick around for an hour, until their mom was ready to leave. They were supposed to sit in the storage room behind the library, reading or doing homework.

The storage room was small and cramped, with bookshelves and stacks of boxes. There were two chairs and a table and one window.

And there was a tall cardboard box that was some kind of time machine.

Other than that, it was a pretty normal room.

Abby was at the table when Doc walked in.

"Any sign of him?" Doc asked.

"Abraham Lincoln?" Abby said. "No. I was hoping he'd be here."

"Yeah," Doc said. "We need to talk to him."

"You think he knows? About Abigail Adams disappearing from the White House?"

"I bet he does. Those history guys all know each other."

A few days before, Abraham Lincoln had jumped out of the tall cardboard box. Really, more like fallen out. Anyway, he'd come

TIME
MACHINE
(YOU WOULD
NEVER GUESS IT)

to say he was sick of kids' complaining about history—he said it hurt his feelings. He'd decided to quit history and become a pro wrestler. It hadn't exactly worked out, and Doc and Abby had convinced him to go back to doing what he was supposed to do.

But other people from history saw what Lincoln did. They realized *they* didn't have to do the same old things over and over, either. So now history was broken. Or very mixed up at least.

Think of the possibilities!

Doc and Abby had promised Lincoln they would help fix it. But how?

Doc stepped over to the cardboard box. It was as tall as he was. He opened one of the top flaps and got up on tiptoes to look in.

"Nope, no Lincoln," Doc said. "Just a few textbooks. And a piece of paper." Doc tilted the box toward the window to let in more light. "Looks like a note."

He crawled in and got the note.

Dear Abby and Doc,

I stopped by this morning, hoping to see you. As you have no doubt realized by now, Abigail Adams is missing. It is quite possible that she has become a pirate. Can you please take care of this? I'd handle it myself, but I'm too busy training for my next wrestling match. Just kidding! I'm actually packing to leave for Washington. Mrs. Lincoln sends her greetings.

Your friend,
A. Lincoln

Doc set the box upright. He stepped onto a chair, then onto a table, then up onto a tall stack of boxes.

"What are you doing?" Abby asked.

"You heard the man," Doc said. "We have to take care of this."

"But wait, let's think for a second," Abby said. "We don't even know how the box works."

"We know how it worked last time," Doc said. "We jumped in, and *boom*! We appeared in, you know, history."

"But it might not—"

"So now we'll go back to Washington in 1800," Doc said. "Find Abigail Adams, fix everything, and be back in time for soccer."

Abby didn't think it would be that simple.

"Look," Doc said, "do you want to fix history or do homework?"

Before Abby could answer, Doc jumped. He soared across the room, hit the top flaps of the box feet first, fell through—and disappeared without a sound.

Abby got up and looked in the box.

20

Nothing down there but a few history textbooks.

"Hold on," Abby said, climbing onto the wobbly stack of boxes.

CHAPTER FOUR

Doc stood up and brushed dirt off his pants. Abby plopped down a few feet away.

"See," Doc said. "Told you it would work."

They were on the side of a muddy road. There were fields, with clumps of trees here and there. And a few half-finished buildings.

In the distance was a building that looked like the picture in their history textbook.

"The White House," Abby said, pointing.

YOU THERE!

a man shouted.

The man was coming toward them, waving. He was average height, a little round around the middle, about sixty-five years old. He was bald except for a puff of white curls above each ear.

"Have you seen Mrs. Adams?" he asked.

"No, sorry," Doc said, "but we just got here. I'm Doc. This is Abby."

"Ah, yes, Abraham Lincoln's friends, the ones who broke history," the man said, shaking their hands.

"Where's your wig?" Doc asked.

"Excuse me, young man?"

"You know," Doc said. "In paintings, you always have that wig. All white, with the funny curls at the bottom."

"I despise that thing," John Adams said. "I wear it to look fancy, but it itches like poison ivy!"

"So how is it being president?" Doc asked. "Pretty fun?"

"It's awful," John moaned. "No matter what I do, people complain. I'll never be re-elected."

"Um, guys," Abby said. "Shouldn't we be looking for Abigail Adams?"

"Ah, Abigail, my wonderful wife, my dearest friend," John said.

One of the few people I know who speaks out against the evil of slavery.

And in favor of more rights for women, she's well known for that.

"She sounds awesome," Abby said.

"Did you know," John said, "when a woman gets married, everything she owns becomes her husband's property. Everything. To do with as he wishes. That's the law."

"No way," Abby said.

"It's true," said the president. "Abigail has often urged me to make laws that are more fair to women. If only I'd listened! We have to find her!"

"We will, we will," Abby said.

"She talked about becoming a pirate, right?" Doc said. "So she'll need to get on a boat. Where's the nearest port?"

"Just down the road here," John said.

They hurried toward the Potomac River. And they had the right idea, but they were looking in the wrong place.

And the wrong time.

———————•———————

At that exact moment, Abigail Adams was on the Caribbean island of Cuba. In the year 1720.

She walked along a waterfront street lined with shops and inns. The sun beat down, and she was starting to cook in her long, heavy dress. She stopped outside a tavern called The Spy-Glass, listening to the lively shouts and songs coming from inside.

Abigail Adams pushed open the door.

It was dark inside, compared with the bright street. Abigail stood in the doorway, blinking.

The singing stopped. Dozens of men turned and stared at the stranger.

Abigail cleared her throat. "Good day, gentlemen," she began. "I was hoping

someone here might be able to tell me where
I can meet a pirate."

The room was silent. For several long
seconds.

And then the place exploded in laughter.

CHAPTER FIVE

A minute later, Abigail sat at a tiny table in the corner of the tavern. The place was again filled with singing and laughter. Across the table sat Anne Bonny, the most feared female pirate of the Caribbean. Bonny was tall and strong, with long red hair. She wore pants and a man's shirt, but was not hiding the fact that she was a woman.

"First off, don't call us pirates," said Bonny. "We prefer 'gentlemen of fortune.'"

"My apologies," Abigail Adams said.

ANNE BONNY. DO NOT MESS WITH HER.

"You know what they do to pirates, right? Heard of Captain Kidd?"

"Hanged, wasn't he?" Abigail asked.

"Hanged, mate, by the Thames River in London," Bonny said. "And they left his body up there to rot as an example to others. Swayed in the breeze a year and more, till the birds picked his bones clean. Sure you don't want some rum?"

"I'm fine."

Bonny lifted her mug and took a swig. A man stumbled past, swaying into Bonny's elbow, splashing rum all over the table.

Bonny stood, grabbed the man by his shirt, and threw him face-first into the wall.

"So you were asking about joining a ship?" Bonny said, sitting back down. "We're sailing tonight. Always need men."

"What about women?"

"Women aboard ships is bad luck, sailors say."

"How silly," Abigail said.

"Aye, but you can win 'em over," Bonny said.

"How?"

"Start out as a man," Bonny said. "In disguise, like. Till they see you can fight. That's what I did." She drained her mug and wiped her mouth with the back of her hand. "The *Revenge* is our ship. Just ask for Captain Rackham."

———•———

"Tell us again," Abby said. "When did you see her last?"

Abby, Doc, and John Adams were in the East Room of the White House. They'd looked for Abigail Adams all over town. No luck.

"This morning. She was hanging clothes to dry," John said, pointing to the shirts and stockings hanging all over the room. The empty laundry basket sat by the wall. "All of a sudden, she starts talking about pirates.

Something about Anne Bonny and the Golden Age of Caribbean pirates."

"The Golden Age, that's *way* before now," Doc said. "The early 1700s, I think. Dad got me that pirate book, remember?"

Doc and Abby's dad was a history teacher. He was always bringing home history books.

"Yeah," Abby said. "I remember how shocked we were that you actually read it."

"Well, it was *good*," Doc said. "Not boring, like history usually is."

"Excuse me?" John Adams said. "Boring?"

"Sorry, sometimes it's good," Doc said. "Is it always so cold in here?"

"I'm afraid so," John said. "What's your sister doing?"

Abby had suddenly started yanking clothes off the strings, tossing them onto the floor.

"I need to clear a path to the basket," she said.

"Careful with those stockings!" John cried.

"I was going to wear those tomorrow."

Abby threw the stockings to John. "The cardboard box works in our storage room, right?" she said.

"Right," Doc said. "Maybe the basket works here."

Abby backed up across the room. She crouched down, like she was about to start a race.

"Okay, um, Basket," Abby said. "I want to find Abigail Adams. I don't know exactly where she is, but if you could take me there, that would be great. Thanks."

She burst into a sprint, jumped high, and flew into the laundry basket.

"Yes!" Doc cheered.

WHOOSH!

John Adams looked in the basket. It was empty. He lifted it. Nothing underneath but solid floor.

"Would you put that down, Mr. President?" Doc asked. "I'm gonna need to jump in."

CHAPTER SIX

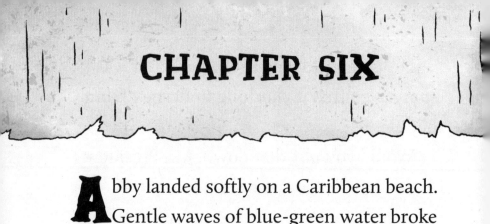

Abby landed softly on a Caribbean beach. Gentle waves of blue-green water broke on the white sand. At a nearby wharf, sailors sang as they loaded goods onto a wooden ship.

Doc came down next to Abby.

"Looks right," she said, standing up.

"It's not Washington, anyway," Doc said.
"How do we find her?"

"I don't know. Let's look around."

Abby helped Doc up, and they walked
along the waterfront street. As they passed a
rope workshop, men looked up and stared.

"I guess we *do* look kind of weird," Abby said.

"Not me," Doc said.

"Our clothes, I mean."

The door of The Spy-Glass tavern opened, and Anne Bonny stepped out.

"Not Abigail Adams," Abby said after Bonny had walked past.

Then a short, gray-haired woman in a long dress came out.

"Could be her," Abby said.

The woman walked along the street, looking in shop windows. She went into a clothing store.

And came out five minutes later in men's clothing—pants and tall boots and a shirt that was way too big. Her hair was tied back in a ponytail.

Would have gotten a parrot—but that seemed a bit **much**.

"Excuse me!" Abby called out. "Are you Abigail Adams?"

"Is it that obvious?" Abigail asked, looking down at her new outfit.

"Only to us," Doc said.

"I'm Abby. This is Doc."

"Yes," Abigail said, "the ones who broke history."

"That's not really fair," Doc complained. "It was just as much Abe Lincoln's fault."

Abigail Adams smiled. "In that case, he did us all a great favor. This is much more fun than my usual job. Good day."

She began walking toward the wharf.

"Hold on!" Abby said, chasing after her. "We're supposed to, you know, save you."

"I don't need to be saved, thank you," Abigail said.

"So it's true?" Doc asked. "You're going to be a pirate?"

"Gentleman of fortune," Abigail said. "The

40

things you learn! I'm to join the crew of a man called Captain Rackham."

"I've read about him," Doc said. "He's known as Calico Jack. Famous for his love of colorful clothes."

Abigail sighed. "You children know more of pirates than you do of my husband. Or me."

"That's not true. We know about you, too," Abby said. "Like how you hang up laundry in the White House."

"Ugh!" Abigail cried.

"What'd I say? Sorry!"

But Abigail Adams was already walking away.

———•———

Out on the wharf, Jack Rackham shouted at his men as they hauled barrels up a gangplank onto their ship. Calico Jack was a powerful man in striped pants and a red coat, with a yellow scarf around his neck.

"Never!" the men shouted, laughing as they worked. They were young men from all over the world.

Abigail Adams walked up and said in a fake deep voice, "I'm looking for Captain Rackham."

Rackham swung around. "Are ye now, old fellow?"

"Yes," Abigail said. "My name's Adams. If you please, I would like to join your crew."

Rackham laughed. "That so? Yer none too young to be sailin' with the likes of we."

"I have heard your ship needs men."

"Not tiny men!" Rackham roared, laughing again. "But true enough, we need hands. So many have run off, so many have gone down to Davy Jones's Locker."

"Why?" Adams asked. "What's in the locker?"

"Means they're dead, mate," Anne Bonny

said, jumping from the ship to the wharf. "Gone to a watery grave."

"As shall we all," Rackham said.

"Beats hangin' from a rope," Bonny said.

"True enough," Rackham agreed. "Can ye cook, Adams?"

"No," she said. "I mean, I *can*, of course. But I've done enough cooking for a lifetime."

"Give him a chance, Jack," Bonny said. "We'll need all the help we can get just to escape from port."

Rackham nodded. "Aye, me wife's right," he said. "Have a look."

He pointed out to the water. Two ships sat in the harbor a few miles from land, blocking the way out to sea. Anne Bonny handed Abigail Adams a spyglass.

Through the glass, Abigail could see the ships clearly. The larger ship's deck was lined with cannons. The big guns were pointed right at Rackham's ship.

"British navy," Rackham explained. "Been hunting us for months. The bigger one's a warship, and the other carries supplies, I reckon. We figure the warship'll start shooting at us any moment."

Abigail lowered the spyglass. She was surprised to see that both Rackham and Bonny were smiling.

"We're trapped," Rackham said.

"But not to worry," Bonny said. "See, we figured us a little plan."

CHAPTER SEVEN

"We need some kind of plan," Doc said.

"A plan would be good," Abby agreed.

They'd just watched Abigail Adams climb aboard Jack Rackham's ship. But there didn't seem to be any way to get onboard without being noticed.

And did they really want to get aboard a pirate ship?

Well, they sort of did. But then what?

"How about this?" Doc said. "We go back— back to the storage room—and we wait for Lincoln and see what he thinks?"

"Makes sense," Abby said. "We're not doing any good here."

"Let's do it," Doc said. "Okay, say it with me. One, two, three . . ."

Together they shouted:

HISTORY IS BORING!

But nothing happened. They didn't disappear.

They shouted it again: "History is boring!"

Still nothing.

"Uh-oh," Doc said.

"Must you keep saying that?" asked a man sitting on a crate, sewing a fishing net.

Don't you know how it hurts our feelings?

"It's not personal, sir," Abby said. "It's sort of a magic spell. Supposed to get us back to our own time."

"At least it did last time," Doc said. "This time, not so magic."

"Well," said the fisherman, "maybe those of us who live here in history are sick of hearing it. Ever think of that?"

The man's face was tilted down, and he had a cap pulled low over his eyes. But there was something familiar about his voice. Also, it really sounded like he was trying not to laugh.

"Is that you, Mr. Lincoln?" Doc asked.

The man looked up from his sewing. He lifted the cap. Yep, it was Abraham Lincoln.

How do you like the beard?

he asked.

"Nice," Abby said. "Is it a disguise?"

"No, it's real," Lincoln said. "I'm about to head to Washington to become president. Supposed to have the beard by the time I get there."

"Good luck," Doc said.

"I'll need it," said Lincoln. "But right now, we have a more pressing problem. Abigail Adams just got onto a pirate ship."

"We saw," Abby said.

"And you need to get her off," Lincoln said.

"Us?" Doc asked.

Lincoln looked around. "I really can't be seen here," he said. "The more I travel around in time, the more jealous everyone else in history gets—and the more they'll want to do it themselves."

"Isn't it dangerous on pirate ships?" Abby asked. "It is in the movies."

"I don't get to watch movies, sadly," Lincoln said.

"Too busy?"

"Yes," said Lincoln. "Plus, they weren't invented when I was alive. But listen, it's *very* dangerous on pirate ships. Especially when they're being hunted by the British navy."

"Rackham and his crew are going to get captured, right?" Doc asked.

Lincoln nodded.

"Put on trial and hanged?"

Lincoln nodded.

That didn't make Abby and Doc feel any better.

"I'll keep an eye on you," Lincoln said, pulling his cap down over his face. "Thanks again for helping."

He picked up the fishing net and went back to his sewing.

CHAPTER EIGHT

Nothing happened until after dark.

It was a moonless night on the coast of Cuba, and the sky and the water were black as ink.

A flash of fire burst from a cannon on the British warship in the harbor. A cannonball screamed through the night toward Jack Rackham's ship and crashed into the wood of the wharf, sending splinters flying. Rackham's ship was still tied up at the wharf. Lights burned in a few lanterns on deck. No people could be seen.

A second cannon fired, then a third, then several at once.

BOOM!

BOOM!

BOOM!

Cannonballs splashed into the water near shore, and hit the sand with heavy thuds, and struck Rackham's ship with earsplitting cracks.

But no one was aboard the pirate ship.

Jack Rackham, Anne Bonny, and the entire crew were crowded aboard two long rowboats. They were gliding slowly and silently across the harbor toward the British ships.

"It's working, boys," Bonny whispered.

There were ten men in the boat with Bonny. If you include Abigail Adams.

Abigail dipped her oar into the water and pulled. She was amazed—the plan really *was* working. The pirates had left lanterns burning aboard Rackham's ship to make it look as if they were still there. The British sailors were so busy firing at the ship, they didn't notice the little boats coming right toward them.

"Steady now," Anne Bonny whispered.

They were right below the bow of the smaller British ship. Jack Rackham, with the rest of the crew, slid up in the other rowboat.

The British warship was anchored about a hundred yards away. It was still blasting its cannons toward shore.

At Bonny's signal, the men pulled out pistols and swords.

Bonny stood, lifting a rope with a grappling hook on the end. She tossed the rope up, and the hook caught on the ship's rail. She pulled out a long knife and held it between her teeth. Then she pulled the rope tight and began to climb.

She swung a leg over the rail

and landed quietly on the deck of the British ship. There were only a few sailors on deck. They were looking toward shore, cheering as cannonballs bashed Rackham's ship to pieces.

One by one, with knives between their teeth, more of Rackham's men climbed aboard. Bonny and the men tiptoed up behind the sailors, their weapons raised in the air.

Bonny said, "Speak a word, and you're all dead men."

The sailors spun around. They were stunned to be facing armed pirates.

"See those boats," Bonny said, pointing to the rowboats she and the crew had arrived in. "You're going to get on those, and you're going to row toward shore. Make a sound, and we blow you out of the water. Clear enough?"

The sailors looked miserable. But they nodded. What choice did they have?

"And, gentlemen," Bonny said, "thankee kindly for the ship."

The sailors climbed down to the boats, and Abigail Adams and Jack Rackham and the rest of the pirate crew climbed aboard the British ship. Now *their* ship.

Rackham swung his sword into the anchor cable, slicing it in two. In just a few minutes, the crew had the ship turned about and sailing out to sea.

No one noticed two nine-year-old kids hanging on to the rope that was still hooked to the ship's rail.

CHAPTER NINE

Abby and Doc had "borrowed" a small boat and followed Rackham's crew to the British ship. They'd managed to grab hold of the rope without being seen.

Now that the ship was moving, they inched up the rope and peeked their heads over the rail.

This might have been a huge mistake.

Shh . . . They'll hear you.

A woman stood at the tiller, her dark hair blowing in the wind. There was no one else in sight.

"Must be Mary Read," Doc whispered. "The other famous woman pirate who sailed with Jack Rackham."

"Where's everyone else?" Abby whispered.

They climbed over the rail and crouched on the dark deck. Doc pointed to an open hatch. Abby nodded.

They stepped down a ladder to the lower level of the ship. Barrels and crates were stacked everywhere, and empty hammocks swayed. They heard voices up ahead, coming from a large cabin.

"Can ye read, Adams?" Jack Rackham asked.

Abby and Doc crept closer and crouched behind a wooden chest. They could see into the cabin. The room was crowded and lit by dozens of candles. Men puffed on pipes and drank from big mugs.

"Of course I can read, Captain Rackham," Abigail Adams said. "I learned to read and write at home and spent countless hours in my father's library. You see, in the colony of Massachusetts, where I grew up, most schools did not admit girls."

"Good," said Calico Jack. "Most of my men can barely—"

"Good, you say?" Abigail interrupted. "Good that schools were not open to girls? How can a country produce smart citizens and leaders except with education?"

"Adams," Anne Bonny cut in, "why are you talking about girls?"

"Girls should have the same chance to go to school as boys," Abigail said. "No issue is more important to me."

"Aye, agreed," Bonny said, "but it's plain to see that *you're* not a girl. Right?"

"Oh, right," Abigail said, her voice suddenly getting much deeper. She shot Bonny a look of thanks.

"Read these here rules, Adams," Rackham

said, tapping his pipe on a sheet of paper. "And sign at the bottom. Or else you're shark bait. Understood?"

"I believe so," Abigail said.

She picked up the paper and read aloud.

"I put that last part in," Rackham said.

"Aren't you clever," said Abigail. "Let's see what else this says. No playing of cards or dice for money."

"To prevent fights," Bonny said.

"No striking one another onboard," Abigail read, "but every man's quarrels to be ended on shore, with swords or pistols. If any man should lose a limb in the service, he is to have eight hundred pieces of eight out of the ship's common stores."

"These are the famous pirate articles," Doc whispered to Abby. "Kind of like laws.

SILVER COIN
(ALSO KNOWN AS "PIECE OF EIGHT" OR "SPANISH DOLLAR")

But for people who don't follow any other laws."

Abigail Adams read the rest of the rules—crew members had to keep their weapons clean and ready at all times. They could be whipped for being careless with fire. No one was allowed to leave the crew, till all had earned at least one thousand pieces of eight. The captain was chosen by vote. Anyone could challenge the captain and demand a new vote. But if you lost the vote, you'd be left to die on a deserted island.

Abigail Adams lifted a feather pen from the table.

"We can't let her sign that," Doc whispered.

Abby stood up. "Hold on, Abigail!" she shouted. "I mean, sorry, Mr. Adams. Don't sign that paper!"

Everyone spun toward Doc and Abby.

"Stowaways!" screeched Jack Rackham.

CHAPTER TEN

That night, while men in hammocks snored all around her, Abigail Adams wrote a letter to her husband.

My dearest friend,

I have done it. I signed the pirate articles and have joined the crew of Captain Jack Rackham. I am disguised as a man, but there are two other women aboard, Anne Bonny, who is quite nice for a pirate, and Mary Read. Bonny and Read enjoy equal rights with the men on the ship.

The other remarkable thing is that two children slipped aboard, those young friends of Abraham Lincoln, the ones who helped him become a professional wrestler. They wish to bring me back to cold and dreary Washington, but I have no desire to go. Why should I? Captain Rackham wanted to throw the children into the sea, but I was able to talk him out of that rash action. I believe they are now tied to the mast on deck, poor dears.

John, you would hate it aboard a pirate ship. The cabins are cramped and smell of feet. My supper tonight was a biscuit with raisins. When the raisins began to move, I realized they were not raisins at all, but live insects. I picked them off my biscuit, but others ate theirs with gusto, declaring the bugs to be "Extra protein!"

CHAPTER ELEVEN

When the sun rose the next morning, Doc and Abby were sitting on deck, fast asleep. They were tied to the mast by a rope wrapped around their chests.

Doc woke up when he felt something poking his leg.

"Cut that out," he said.

"What?" asked Abby, opening her eyes.

"Quit tickling my leg."

"I'm not."

"Someone is," Doc said. "Or something. Oh, I see now, it's just rats." Then, realizing what he'd just said, he yelped,

He wriggled his legs, and a few rats scurried away.

"Oh, gross!" Abby said, checking her legs for rats.

"Most ships have far more rats aboard than people," Abigail Adams said, walking up. "How are you two this morning?"

"We've been better," Doc said.

"No doubt," said Abigail. She handed Abby a jug of water. Abby drank, and then handed it to Doc.

"What will Rackham do to us?" Abby asked. "Make us walk the plank?"

"That's just a movie thing," Doc said. "Real-life pirates didn't waste time with stuff like that. They'd just throw you overboard."

"Is that supposed to make me feel better?"

"No one's going overboard," Abigail Adams said. "I won't allow it."

"Thanks," Doc said, "but *we're* supposed to be saving *you*."

Abigail smiled. "And you're doing a splendid job." She pulled out a knife and cut the rope holding them to the mast.

Doc and Abby stood just as Jack Rackham strode up.

"Well, well, how are my little stowaways this fine mornin'?" Rackham called. "How'd ye fancy a swim with the sharks?"

"Not so much," Doc said.

Rackham laughed. But his eyes weren't smiling. He grabbed Doc's shirt. "I don't allow no children aboard, see? Got no use for 'em!"

"Give them a chance, Captain," Abigail said. "You said yourself we're short of hands."

"What can ye do?" Rackham demanded of Doc.

"I'm pretty good at soccer," Doc said.

"Can ye climb?"

"Sure," Doc said. "Our gym teacher, Mr. Biddle, set up this rope in—"

"Good! Get up to the crow's nest!"

"The what?"

"Crow's nest," Abigail Adams said. "See

71

that basket at the top of the tallest mast?"

Doc looked up—way, way up—at the rocking, swaying, teeny tiny basket.

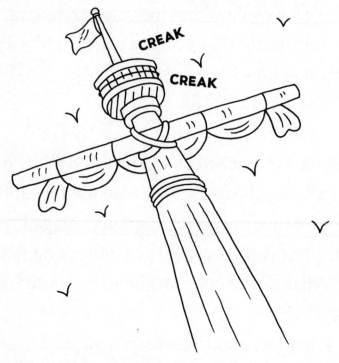

Doc gulped. "I don't know . . ."

Rackham laughed. "Yo ho, a landlubber are ye?"

"Well, now that you mention it," Doc said, "I do love land."

"Not *love*, *lub*!" Rackham screamed.

"Land*lubber*. Means y'ain't been to sea, ye scurvy dog!"

"Captain Rackham," snapped Abigail Adams, "there's no need for that kind of language."

Rackham spun to face Abigail. He towered over her, glaring down.

She stared right back.

Calico Jack lowered his eyes and turned to Doc. "Get up there and watch for ships, see?"

"I'm kind of hungry," Doc said.

"Take this." Rackham held out a biscuit with raisins. The raisins were moving. "And call out loud when ye spots sails."

Doc put the biscuit in his pocket, reached up, and climbed into the rigging. "Hey, this is fun," he said. "Kind of like the world's most dangerous playground."

Rackham yelled, "Be smart now, before I feed ye to the fish!"

"Okay, okay," Doc said. And he climbed higher.

———————•———————

Off the coast of Cuba, the men of the British warship woke to find themselves alone in the harbor. The smaller British supply ship was gone.

The captain roared at his men for falling for the pirates' trick. No one dared point out that *he* was the one who was supposed to be in charge.

"Well, never mind, men," growled the captain. "We'll catch up with them soon enough.

They can't have gotten far.

CHAPTER TWELVE

Doc stood in the crow's nest—basically just a basket with low sides. The views of the sky and ocean were amazing. But the tiny basket dipped and swayed like an amusement park ride that was missing a few parts.

Pretty soon, Doc started to turn green.

Down on deck, Abby had been put to work as a "swabbie." As far as she could tell, the job was to mop the deck and get yelled at.

Doc's stomach gurgled. The

biscuit he'd nibbled was foaming up in his belly. His head was swimming. His face was hot. He felt like he was about to—

Doc shouted.

"Look out, men!" cried Captain Rackham. "Ship in sight! Prepare for battle!"

Doc shouted, "No, I mean—look out!"

And he barfed.

The wind blew it far out to sea. No one on deck even seemed to notice.

Anne Bonny had a spyglass to her eye, searching the horizon. "He's right!" she shouted. "Sail ho! East-southeast!"

Doc looked around. There really was a ship.

"Looks like an unarmed sloop!" Bonny
called out. "Flying a French flag!"

"Raise our French flag!" Rackham called out.
"Ready the cannons! Arm yourselves, men!"

"Can I come down now?" Doc asked.

No one answered. So he started to climb
down.

Men raced around the deck and shouted
commands. A French flag rose high up the

mast and flapped in the wind.

Doc jumped down to the deck, right next to Abby. "Classic pirate trick," he said. "Pretend to be a friendly ship so the other guys let you get close."

"Doesn't seem fair," Abby said.

"I don't think pirates were that into fairness," Doc said.

Abigail Adams hurried over to them. "Quick, children, hide below deck," she said, pointing to an open hatch.

"What are *you* going to do?" Abby asked.

"I'm not sure," Abigail said. "To be honest, I know very little about sword-fighting."

Abby tried to smile. "Beats hanging laundry in the White House, at least. Right?"

Abigail nodded.

But for the first time since becoming a pirate, she looked worried.

———•———

"Raise high the Jolly Roger!" Rackham hollered.

The French flag came down, and Rackham's pirate flag went up—a black flag with a white skull, and swords crossed beneath the skull. Every sailor knew exactly what it meant. No quarter. No mercy. Surrender without a fight—or else!

They call me Jolly Roger, but there's **nothing** jolly about me.

"Y'are in range of our guns!" Rackham shouted to the French trading ship. He waved a sword above his head. Pistols and daggers stuck out of his belt and hung from the sash around his chest. "Give up now, and ye'll not be harmed! But choose to fight, and every one of ye must expect immediate death!"

Standing beside him were Anne Bonny and Mary Read, loaded with weapons. Four pirates hung in the rigging, aiming muskets. The rest lined the side of the ship, shouting rude insults—stuff we can't really print here.

"Hold your fire!" the merchant captain called. "We surrender!"

This is how most pirate attacks went. Merchant captains weren't paid enough to risk their lives battling pirates. They usually let the pirates take what they wanted and went on their way.

Bonny and Read threw grappling hooks over to the other ship. They tugged on the ropes, lashing the two ships together. Then Bonny and Read leaped over six feet of open water, landing on the deck of the captured ship.

"We surrender!" the captain said again.

"We surrender!" called a few other crew members.

"No, we do not surrender!" one man on the merchant ship told Bonny and Read. "We most certainly do not! I demand to speak to your captain!"

The man was not armed. He was average height, a little round around the middle, about sixty-five years old. He wore a white wig with curls on the bottom. His face was red with fury.

Abigail Adams leaped across to the merchant ship and walked up to her husband.

"John," she said. "What are you doing here?"

CHAPTER THIRTEEN

"**H**ey, that's too tight!" howled John Adams.

"Hold still, prisoner!" Anne Bonny commanded.

Bonny held John's arms behind his back while Mary Read tied a rope around his wrists.

"Wait here," Bonny commanded, shoving John to his knees.

Abigail helped him up.

"I have come to rescue you!" John Adams declared.

Abigail Adams sighed. "First the children, and now you. Who says I need rescuing?"

"My dear, you're sailing with savages! Chased by the British navy, rumor has it! I say, you there!" Adams shouted to Jack Rackham. "Are you the captain of that filthy pirate vessel? In the name of the president of the United States, I order you to drop your weapons!"

"And I order ye to hold your tongue," Rackham growled. "If you wish to keep it!"

"I wish to," John said. "But I must insist that you unhand my wife."

"Wife? Who's yer wife?"

"That would be me," Abigail said in her normal voice.

She reached behind her head and untied
her ponytail. She shook her head, and her
gray hair fell around her shoulders.

"Blimey, but I figured as much," Rackham
said, grinning. "Well, makes no difference,

Adams. You're a good man all the same."

"Thank you," she said. "I suppose."

"How about ye?" Rackham said to John. "We take men with skills, see? Force 'em to join us. What can ye do?"

"I'm a lawyer," John said. "Ever heard of Harvard?"

"Carpenter?" Rackham demanded. "Navigator? Surgeon? Cook?"

"I served in Congress during the American Revolution and helped write the Declaration of Independence. Everyone thinks Thomas Jefferson wrote it, but I did quite a bit. You know that part where it says—"

"That a wig ye be wearin'? Give it here!"

Rackham ripped the white wig off John Adams's head.

"Look at me!" Rackham sang, placing the wig on his own head. "I served in Congress! I be friends with Timothy Jefferson!"

The captain danced down the deck as the other pirates laughed and hooted.

Abigail Adams looked at her husband, shaking her head.

John shrugged. "I was only trying to help, dear."

Doc and Abby peeked up from the open hatch.

They were alone on Rackham's ship. They walked to the rail and looked across to the captured ship. All the passengers and crew were tied up. The pirates were searching them for valuables, reaching into pockets, yelping they'd stab anyone who dared to keep anything hidden.

"Let's review," Doc said. "We're stuck in history, with no clue how to leave."

"Check," Abby said.

"The British are hunting us, and, hold on—what do they do to kid pirates? I don't think my book mentioned."

"Let's not find out," Abby said.

"Then we need to get out of here, fast," Doc said. "And somehow save Abigail Adams."

"And John Adams, too!"

"John? Why?" Doc asked. "Isn't he back at the White House?"

"I don't think so," Abby said. "Look!"

There, on the other ship, sitting on a crate with his hands tied behind his back, was the second president of the United States.

Doc and Abby jumped across to the captured ship—where the pirate party was getting started. The pirates had stolen clothes and were parading around in fancy hats and colorful coats and high-heeled boots. They knocked the tops off bottles of wine with the blades of their swords—no time to bother with corkscrews. They cracked open barrels and blasted the locks off chests with their pistols. Coins and jewelry went into a box, to be divvied up later. Stuff they didn't want they carried to the rail and dropped into the ocean.

Doc and Abby helped John Adams to his feet. Doc jumped behind him and started loosening the ropes. Abby looked around. All over the deck, pirates were dancing and singing and tossing stuff into the sea.

But no sign of Abigail Adams.

CHAPTER FOURTEEN

"**W**here is she?" Abby asked.

"Ah, bless you, young man," John said to Doc as the ropes fell from his wrists. "Last I saw Abigail, she was following Captain Rackham. Trying to stop him from hurting any of the prisoners. What a wonderful woman!"

"We have to find her," Abby said. "Maybe we can all get onto a lifeboat or something. Get away while the pirates are too busy to notice."

"This is our chance," Doc said. "Let's go!"

They scrambled down a ladder to the lower deck and started searching the cabins.

At least, Doc and Abby were searching. John Adams was lost in his own thoughts.

"She is a woman who thinks only of the welfare of others," he said.

"We get that," Doc said. "Would you mind helping us find her?"

"I'll tell you a little story," John said.

"Can it wait?" asked Abby.

It couldn't.

"In the spring of 1776, I was in Philadelphia, serving in Congress," John began. "Should we declare independence from Britain? That was the big debate. Many were scared to do so—but not my wife. She wrote to me, urging bold action."

"I long to hear that you have declared an independency—and, by the way, in the new code of laws which I suppose it will be necessary for you to make, I desire you would Remember the Ladies."

"Good stuff," Abby said.

"Her most famous letter," said John. "She knew the United States would need new laws, and she wanted them to be fair to women."

"So did you?" Doc asked. "Remember the ladies?"

"I'm afraid not," John said. "I treated Abigail's letter as a joke. I wrote back that she was 'saucy.'"

"Not cool," Abby said.

"No, dear," said Abigail Adams. "It most certainly was not."

She was standing in front of them in the narrow passageway, hands on her hips.

"Talk it over later, you two," Abby said. "Right now we need to get away from the pirates."

"Why not hide here, on this ship?" Doc suggested. "Wait till Rackham sails away, and then—I don't know, but at least we won't be around when the British show up."

"Smart," Abby said, looking around. "Quick, let's find somewhere to hide!"

They raced down the passageway—and crashed into Jack Rackham.

"Goin' somewhere?" he growled.

Abby smiled. "We were just, you know, uh . . ."

Trying to change the subject, Doc said, "What happened to the wig?"

Rackham rubbed his head. The white wig was gone. "Too itchy!"

"Isn't it?" John Adams said. "Some say they look well, but—"

"Adams!" Rackham cut in.

"Yes?" John asked.

"Not ye!" Rackham screamed. "Ye flea-ridden scalawag!"

Abigail said, "Mr. Rackham, I've spoken to you about that kind of language."

"Apologies," Rackham said. "But I was talking to ye, Adams. Ye signed the articles.

96

Won't be going nowhere." Putting his arm around Doc's shoulder, he added, "And neither can I part with ye! My very best lookout!"

"Funny story." Doc laughed. "The thing is, when I said, 'Look out!' I was actually about to—"

"And my best swabbie!" Rackham said to Abby. "Get back to the ship, all three o' ye!"

"I'm coming too," John Adams announced.

"No, thanks all the same," Rackham said.

"You were asking before about skills," John said. "Well, I have them."

"Such as?" Rackham asked.

"Well . . ." John said. "Such as . . . such as cooking!"

Abigail Adams choked back a laugh.

"Good, I'm starved!" Rackham snapped. "Back to our ship! All four of ye!"

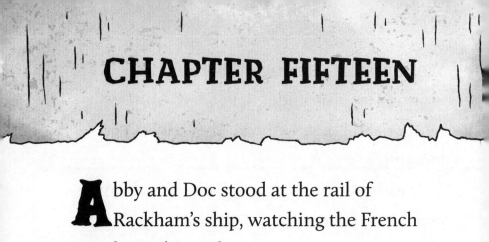

CHAPTER FIFTEEN

Abby and Doc stood at the rail of Rackham's ship, watching the French merchant ship sail away.

"Eagle eye!" Jack Rackham shouted, slapping Doc hard on the back. "I told ye to get up to the nest! Keep a sharp look out—and take this here."

Rackham held out a spyglass. Doc stuck it in his back pocket and started climbing.

"Pirates seem so cool in books," Abby said. "And movies. But you pretty much just go around stealing stuff."

"That's the basic idea," Rackham grunted.

"And acting like slobs," Doc added from a few feet above the deck.

"Up to the nest!" Rackham roared.

"Okay, take it easy," Doc said.

"And ye, swabbie," Rackham growled to Abby. "Get yer mop and wash the poop deck."

"Gross!" Abby said. "No way."

Doc stopped climbing. "It's not what you think," he said. "The toilets are in the bow, the very front of the ship. Two square boxes, open right down to the water."

NOTICE

PIRATES
MUST WASH
HANDS BEFORE
RETURNING TO
PLUNDERING

"Yuck."

"I know," Doc said, "but that way the wind blows the, you know, smell away from the ship."

"Up!" Rackham roared.

"I tried it," Doc said. "The waves slash up and tickle you. Plus, I was afraid I'd get a splinter."

"Up!" Rackham roared.

"Okay, okay, I'm going."

Abby watched her brother climb higher and higher. She was worried for him. And for

100

herself. And Abigail Adams. And John Adams, who'd been sent to the galley to make stew.

———•———

Abby was mopping the deck when Abigail Adams walked up.

"Are you all right, dear?" Abigail asked.

"Fine, thanks," Abby said. "But shouldn't you leave? Before it's too late?"

"I wouldn't mind," Abigail said. "I've had my adventure."

"You know how to leave, right?" Abby asked. "I mean, get back to your own time?"

"I have a general idea," Abigail explained. "I saw what Abraham Lincoln did. And I figured out it had something to do with jumping into, well, *something*. That's why I tried the laundry basket in the White House. I'm hoping the same basic idea will work again."

Abby bent down and emptied a wooden crate of ropes and scraps of sailcloth. Then she jumped in.

"Nope," Abby said. "Still here."

"We'll figure it out, don't worry," Abigail said.

But she seemed a little worried.

Abby got out of the crate and picked up her mop. "So were you mad at John?" she asked. "For laughing at your idea of making laws fairer to women?"

"I certainly was," Abigail said. "In some ways, I have more freedom on this pirate ship than in my own country." Her eyes opened wide, and she shouted,

That's it!

"What?"

"You've just given me an idea," Abigail said. "I know how to get us off this ship!"

CHAPTER SIXTEEN

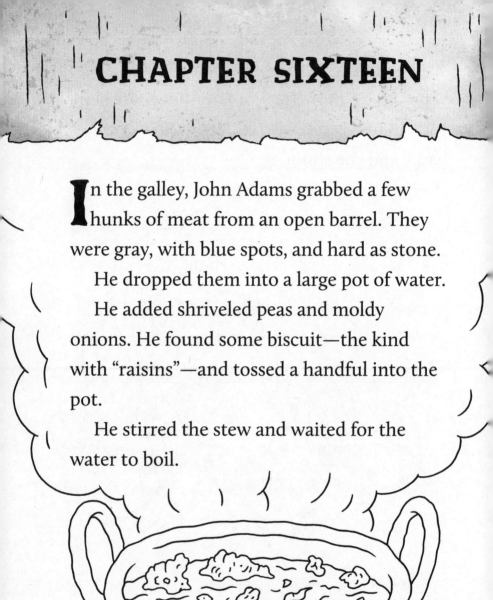

In the galley, John Adams grabbed a few hunks of meat from an open barrel. They were gray, with blue spots, and hard as stone.

He dropped them into a large pot of water.

He added shriveled peas and moldy onions. He found some biscuit—the kind with "raisins"—and tossed a handful into the pot.

He stirred the stew and waited for the water to boil.

Doc was up in the crow's nest, with the spyglass to his eye.

"Uh-oh," he muttered. "That can't be good."

He could see, far in the distance, a ship.

A ship with a British flag.

"Look out!" Doc shouted. "I mean, sails ahoy, or whatever."

He looked down to the deck. The crew members were lying around, sleeping off the effects of their pirate party. It didn't look like anyone had heard him.

Except for his sister and Abigail Adams. They were signaling for him to be quiet and to come down. Doc scurried down the rigging and reported on what he'd seen. Abigail put her arms around the two kids.

"We have even less time than we thought," she told them. "This little ship is no match for the British navy. We'd all be captured— assuming we survived the battle."

"So what do we do?" Doc asked.

"Follow my lead," Abigail said. "Now, where's Captain Rackham?"

They searched the deck. They found Rackham fast asleep with his head on a cannonball.

Abigail nudged him with her foot.

"Noooo," Rackham moaned in his sleep.

Abigail nudged him again. Sort of kicked him. "Wake up, Captain!"

He opened his eyes.

"Captain Rackham," Abigail said. "The pirate code states that any crew member can challenge the captain."

"Aye, it's true, but—"

"Any man, or woman, can say, 'I should be

the new captain!' And demand a vote. And if she wins, she's the captain. Correct?"

"Aye." Rackham yawned. "But I wouldn't—"

Abigail Adams raised her arm and shouted, "I challenge you, Captain Rackham. I say that I would make a better captain!"

Anne Bonny walked up.

"Rules is rules, Jack," she said. "We have to hear her out. But if she loses the vote, well, you know."

That made Jack Rackham laugh.

Doc and Abby looked at each other. They really hoped Abigail Adams knew what she was doing.

CHAPTER SEVENTEEN

The crew gathered in the great cabin. Pirates yawned and held matches to their pipes. Jack Rackham and Anne Bonny sat at the table in the front of the room.

Doc and Abby watched from the back.

"Ye know why we're here," Rackham began. "Adams, say what ye have to say."

Abigail Adams stood and faced the crew.

"Thank you, gentlemen," she said, "and ladies, for your kind attention."

Someone let out a thunderous belch.

"What I wish to say is this," Abigail continued. "Many of you have been pirates for quite some time. Yes, yes, I know you do not like that word, *pirates*. But let's be honest, shall we?"

"Where's supper!" someone demanded.

"It's coming," Anne Bonny called. "Adams, be quick."

"Right," Abigail said. "I wish to suggest a new idea. We give up attacking ships, robbing others, taking things that do not belong to us. And instead, we turn our ship into a school!"

For once, the crew was silent.

"A floating school!" Abigail sang. "Open
to men and women alike. I can be one of
the teachers. And we will invite other pirate
crews to come and join us! We'll study
reading, writing, mathematics, history—
imagine the fun!"

Doc looked at Abby. Abby just shrugged.

"Now I get a turn," Jack Rackham growled.

The crew cheered.

Rackham stood and held out his arms. "Who's been bringin' ye prize after prize? Calico Jack, that's who! We stay on the attack, says I! A merry life and a short one! Who's with me?"

The pirates leaped to their feet and roared.

Abigail Adams said, "So, just to be clear, how many votes for the floating school?"

Abigail raised her own hand. She was the only one. Everyone was glaring at her.

Gulp. Is it getting warm in here all of a sudden?

She shot a look at Doc and Abby.
Very slowly, they raised their hands.

"Traitors!" someone shouted.

"Bilge rats!"

"How could ye, laddies!" Rackham wailed.
"And ye, Adams, I took ye in! Gave ye a taste
o' the good life! And ye stab me in the back!"

"Easy now, Jack," Anne Bonny said. "She
was within her rights to try. And the rules is
clear." Turning to Abigail, she said, "Adams,
ye and anyone who voted with ye, is to be
marooned on a deserted island."

"No!" Abigail Adams cried.

"Aye, left to rot in the sun," Bonny insisted. "Rules is rules."

Abigail lowered her head. "Very well. Rules is rules."

"That was her plan?" Doc whispered to Abby. "Get us all kicked off the ship?"

"Guess so," Abby whispered. "Brilliant!"

"Supper time!"

That was John Adams. He staggered in, groaning with effort, a pot of steaming stew in his hands.

Hot . . . stuff . . . coming . . . through.

Rackham banged the table. "Set it here, cook, I'm starved!"

John put down the pot.

Rackham sniffed the stew and winced. "Did ye boil me shoe in here?"

"I most certainly did not," John said.

The whole cabin was filling with foul-smelling steam. Doc pinched his nose.

Rackham scooped up a spoonful of stew.
He brought it to his lips and slurped.

Then he sprayed it all over his crew.

"Do you think it needs salt?" John asked.

Bonny dipped a spoon into the pot and sipped. She gagged and pounded the table.

John frowned. "It's not easy, you know, cooking for a large group such as this."

"Believe me, I know," Abigail said.

"Ye, cook!" Bonny shouted. "Yer goin' with Adams and the little ones!"

"Going where, sir?" John asked.

"To be marooned on an island!" Rackham bawled.

"Now!" Bonny added. "Before you can cook us anything else!"

Abigail smiled. That wasn't part her of plan. Just a lucky break.

CHAPTER EIGHTEEN

Rackham's ship anchored near a tiny
island—nothing more than a strip of
sand with a few palm trees.

Doc stood on the deck, looking through the spyglass. The British ship was still far off but sailing toward them. *If Rackham finds out*, Doc thought, *he'll make everyone stay and help with the coming battle.*

"What d'ye see?" Rackham demanded.

"Uh, I think a whale," Doc said. "Ooops."

And he dropped the spyglass into the ocean.

"Fool!"

"All ready, Captain!" called one of the pirates.

The crew had lowered a lifeboat to the water and hung a rope ladder off the side of the ship. Abby and Doc climbed down to the lifeboat, followed by Abigail and John Adams.

Then came Jack Rackham and Anne Bonny. Each holding two long swords.

"We'll row ye to the island," Bonny said. She picked up the oars and began to row.

"Kind of you," Abigail said. "Might I ask what the swords are for?"

Rackham smiled. "The duel," he said.

"I see," Abigail said. "And who exactly will be dueling?"

"We will," Rackham snarled. "I like ye, Adams, but ye challenged me, afore the whole crew. I need to make an example of ye, see?"

"And I will be dueling you," Anne Bonny said to John Adams.

"Me?" John asked. "What for?"

"For the stew," Bonny said.

Rackham grunted a laugh.

John looked hurt. "I did my best with very limited ingredients."

"Captain, this is hardly necessary," Abigail

said. "Surely it is punishment enough to be left on a desert island without food or water. Let us part as friends."

Bonny kept rowing. Rackham kept smiling.

Abby leaned toward Abigail Adams. "Was this part of your plan?"

Abigail shook her head. "I was just trying to get us off the ship."

"It worked," Abby said. "And thanks. Only now you have to fight a duel."

"So it appears."

"Well," said Abby, "you *did* say women should be able to do anything men do."

"Perhaps," Abigail said, "but some things men do are just plain stupid."

"Here we is!" Rackham called as the boat slid up onto the beach. "Everyone out!"

Rackham and Bonny carried the swords onto the island. Each took one. The other two they stabbed into the sand.

"Take yer pick!" Rackham said.

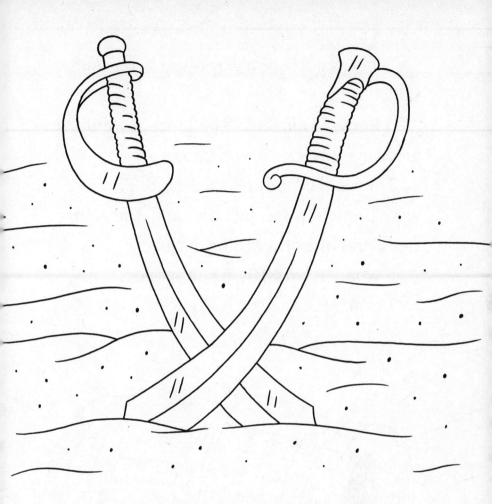

Abigail and John looked at each other.

"Which one do you want, dear?" John asked.

"I'm not sure it matters," Abigail said.

No one was paying attention to Abby and Doc.

"There's gotta be a way outta here," Abby said.

"I know," Doc said. "Abe Lincoln wouldn't just leave us here to, you know . . ."

They looked around the island. There wasn't much to see. Just the sand, the palm trees, and one other thing: a barrel.

A wooden barrel, lying on its side.

Abby lifted it up. It had no top. It was empty.

Looks like a normal barrel, she thought. *But the cardboard box in the storage room behind the library looks pretty normal, too. And the laundry basket in the White House.*

"You thinking what I'm thinking?" Abby asked.

Doc nodded. "Worth a shot."

Rackham and Bonny started warming up, dancing around each other, clanging their swords together.

"Bet I win my duel quicker than you, Jack!" Bonny bragged.

"Yer on!" Rackham cackled. "Fifty pieces of eight for the winner!"

"Agreed!" Bonny said. "Pay me when we get back to the ship."

"Not likely, Annie!"

The other two swords were still sticking

up out of the sand. Abigail and John were still standing next to them.

"Go on, take 'em!" Rackham demanded, waving his sword in the air. "Time to fight!"

CHAPTER NINETEEN

"**G**uys!" Abby shouted. "Over here!"

"Quick!" Doc yelled, "Jump in!"

They tilted the top of the empty barrel toward Abigail and John.

Abigail looked over. "You first, children!"

"We're fine," Abby said. "We'll be right behind you. You need to hurry!"

Abigail looked at Jack Rackham, who was swinging his sword in the air.

> It slices! It dices! It purees my enemies!

"Yes, it looks as if we do," she said. "Come along, John!"

She turned and ran toward the barrel.

"Get back here!" Rackham yelped. "Ye can't hide from Calico Jack!"

Abigail jumped and flew into the barrel—

and was gone.

John Adams ran up a second later—and slid to a stop in front of the barrel.

"What are you doing?" Doc asked.

"Promise you will remember Abigail," John said. "And not just about the laundry in the White House."

"We promise," Abby said, "but hurry!"

Rackham was prowling toward them.

"Don't make the same mistake I did," John urged. "Remember!"

He jumped into the barrel—and was gone.

Rackham raged forward, raising his sword.

"No, don't!" Doc cried.

But he did—he swung his blade into the side of the barrel. Pieces of wood went flying. There was nothing left of the barrel.

"We were still using that," Doc said.

"Where'd they go?" Rackham bawled.

"Bring 'em back, ye little!—"

Abby snatched up a handful of sand and tossed it into Rackham's eyes.

"Run!" she shouted.

She and Doc took off running, stumbling in the loose sand. There was nowhere to hide. Rackham and Bonny chased them around the tiny island and were gaining on them, until—

The pirates skidded to a stop. They looked out at the water, where the sound had come from.

The British warship was firing its cannons at Rackham's ship.

A cannonball sailed toward the pirate ship and plopped into the sea. The British guns were not quite in range yet.

"Blow me down!" Rackham bawled.

"To the ship, Jack!" Bonny cried. "We'll fight 'em off yet!"

The pirates raced to the rowboat, pushed it into the shallow water, jumped in, and rowed furiously toward their ship.

Abby and Doc stood on the beach, panting.

———•———

The battle was over quickly.

Jack Rackham and Anne Bonny made it back to their ship in time to put up a fight. But Bonny and Mary Read were the only ones fighting. The rest of the crew, including Jack Rackham, disappeared below deck. The British stormed aboard Rackham's ship, took everyone prisoner, and lowered Calico Jack's pirate flag.

Abby and Doc watched the whole thing from the desert island.

Their new home.

Doc tried to look on the bright side. "At least we got off the pirate ship in time."

"Yeah," Abby said, "and we saved Abigail Adams. And John. At least, I think we did."

"Let's hope," Doc said. "Is that a rowboat coming toward us?"

"Looks like it."

And it was. A small boat, rowed by one man. The rower was wearing a black jacket and tall hat. But his back was to the beach, so Abby and Doc couldn't see who it was.

"What if it's a British sailor?" Doc wondered. "Coming to arrest us?"

"We'll claim the pirates captured us," Abby said. "Forced us to serve with them."

"That's what pirates always said when they got caught."

"Did it work?" Abby asked.

"Nope."

"Got a better idea?" Abby asked.

"Nope."

"Here he comes," Abby said. "That hat looks familiar."

The bottom of the boat hit the sand and stopped. The rower stood, lifted a long, thin leg—and toppled into the shallow sea.

He stood, water streaming off his black suit. He fished his hat out of the water and put it on. He splashed up onto the beach.

"Boy, are we glad to see you," Doc said.

"Good to see you, too," said Abraham Lincoln.

CHAPTER TWENTY

They sat together on the beach—Doc,
Abby, and Abraham Lincoln.

Lincoln said,

A general I knew once told me, "Sir, I have as brave a heart as anyone.

But when danger nears, my legs turn cowardly and run away, taking my brave heart with 'em."

Lincoln laughed his high-pitched laugh.
Doc and Abby just sat there.

"You still don't like my jokes, I see," Lincoln said.

"No offense," Abby said, "but it's hard to tell that they're jokes."

"In any case," Lincoln said. "You showed brave hearts. And legs. You did very well."

"We did it again," Doc said. "We fixed history!"

Lincoln sighed. "Nothing's fixed, I'm afraid. Don't you see? The cat's out of the bag."

"Now everyone from history knows they can do whatever they want," Abby said. "Why should you and Abigail Adams get to have all the fun?"

"Exactly what I'm worried about," Lincoln said. "I have a feeling history is about to get a lot more mixed up. Can we keep it from twisting completely out of control? That's the question."

"We'll help if we can," Doc said.

"You know where to find us," Abby said.

"Good. I'll be counting on you." Lincoln stood and stretched. "I better get going."

Abby said, "Um, aren't you forgetting something?"

"Something kind of important?" said Doc.

"Oh, yes, of course." Lincoln touched his chin. "How do you like my new beard?"

"You showed us already," Doc said.

"So I did," Lincoln said. "I suppose you meant, how do you get home?"

"You do know, don't you?" Abby asked.

"This is all very new, but I understand a little more than I did before," Lincoln said. "It will be different every time, the words you need to leave history."

"What are they this time?" Doc asked. "Wait—you think John Adams was trying to tell us? Before jumping in the barrel?"

Abby's face lit up. "Right! He kept telling us to remember Abigail! The stuff she did, the important stuff. Like that famous letter about women's rights. Could *that* be it?"

"Oh, yeah, that was great," Doc said. And he shouted: "Remember the women!"

Nothing happened.

"No," Abby said, "it was

REMEMBER THE *LADIES*!

And they vanished.

———————•———————

And reappeared in the cardboard box in the storage room behind the library of their school. They tipped the box over and crawled out.

Abby set the box upright. Doc grabbed a copy of their history textbook from the shelf.

He flipped to the page about Abigail Adams in the White House. She was there.

But not for long.

"John Adams was right," Doc said. "He lost the next election."

He read aloud:

Thomas Jefferson became the third president.

Abigail and John headed home to their Massachusetts farm to enjoy a long retirement together.

Today, Abigail Adams is remembered as a smart and brave patriot, a woman whose ideas about equality for all Americans were ahead of their time.

"Sounds right," Abby said.

"Yeah, for now," Doc said.

"I know. Who do you think will be next to, you know, escape from history?"

"Could be anyone," Doc said.

He started flipping pages in the textbook. Abby looked over his shoulder.

"Wait," Abby said, pointing to a page, "that can't be right."

"Where? Oh, I see it." Doc laughed. "Wait till Lincoln sees!"

The door opened.

Abby and Doc's mom stuck her head in.

You guys ready?

They put down the textbook and grabbed their bags.

"Get your homework done?" their mom asked as they walked to the parking lot.

"Not exactly," Doc said.

"What? You had an hour! What were you doing?"

"Working on this, um, new project," Abby said.

"History project," Doc added.

"History!" Their mom was shocked. "Your dad will be thrilled. Want to grab some pizza before soccer practice?"

"Yeah," Abby said. "I'm really hungry."

"Feels like we haven't eaten in days," Doc said.

Their mom laughed. "All right, but just one slice each. Dad's cooking dinner. He's making his famous stew. With biscuits!"

Doc and Abby looked at each other.

They shrugged and got into the car.

UN-TWISTING HISTORY

I'm sure you realize that a lot of this story is made up—Abigail Adams never jumped into a laundry basket at the White House and appeared in the Caribbean, for example. She never served on a pirate ship. Still, a lot of what's in the book is true.

There really were female pirates, and we know for a fact that Anne Bonny and Mary Read sailed with "Calico Jack" Rackham. Bonny and Rackham really were married. The scene where they steal a ship and escape (Chapter Eight) is based on a story that has been told about Rackham and Bonny for nearly three hundred years. The "pirate articles" that crew members had to sign are real. And the details of what life was like on a pirate ship, and what pirate attacks were like, are also based on reliable sources.

Rackham's ship was hunted by the British, and the final showdown took place in October 1720 off the coast of Jamaica. Bonny and Read put up a fight, but the rest of the crew was either too scared or too drunk to join the battle. Everyone was captured, thrown into prison, and sentenced to death. Bonny had no sympathy for her husband. "Had you fought like a man," she told Rackham, "you need not have been hanged like a dog."

Rackham and the other men in his crew were hanged. Mary Read died in prison. No one knows what happened to Anne Bonny.

Would Abigail Adams have known about Anne Bonny?

I like to think so, and it's actually quite possible. A book called *A General History of the Robberies and Murders of the Most Notorious Pyrates*, published in England in 1724, helped

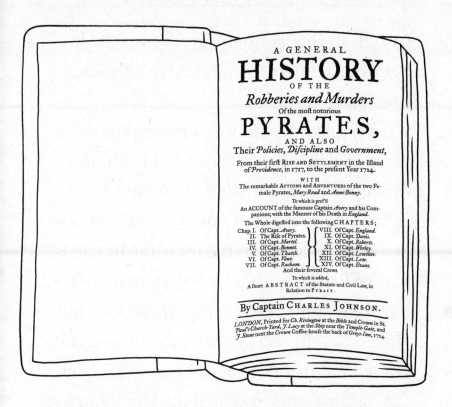

A GENERAL

HISTORY

OF THE

Robberies and Murders

Of the moſt notorious

PYRATES,

AND ALSO

Their *Policies, Diſcipline* and *Government,*

From their firſt RISE AND SETTLEMENT in the Iſland
of *Providence,* in 1717, to the preſent Year 1724.

WITH

The remarkable ACTIONS and ADVENTURES of the two Female Pyrates, *Mary Read* and *Anne Bonny.*

To which is pref'd

An ACCOUNT of the famous Captain *Avery* and his Com-
panions; with the Manner of his Death in *England.*

The Whole digeſted into the following CHAPTERS;

Chap. I. Of Capt. *Avery.*   VIII. Of Capt. *England.*
II. The Riſe of Pyrates.   IX. Of Capt. *Davis.*
III. Of Capt. *Martel.*   X. Of Capt. *Roberts.*
IV. Of Capt. *Bonnet.*   XI. Of Capt. *Worley.*
V. Of Capt. *Thatch.*   XII. Of Capt. *Lowther.*
VI. Of Capt. *Vane.*   XIII. Of Capt. *Low.*
VII. Of Capt. *Rackam.*   XIV. Of Capt. *Evans.*

And their ſeveral Crews

To which is added,

A ſhort ABSTRACT of the Statute and Civil Law, in
Relation to PYRACY.

By Captain CHARLES JOHNSON.

LONDON, Printed for *Ch. Rivington* at the *Bible* and *Crown* in St.
Paul's Church-Yard, J. Lacy at the *Ship* near the *Temple-Gate,* and
J. Stone next the *Crown* Coffee-houſe the back of *Greys-Inn,* 1724.

make Bonny famous. Abigail Smith (as she
was then called) was born twenty years later,
in 1744, in Massachusetts. Abigail had no
formal education, but she learned to read
and write at home and loved to learn about
history. Maybe she came across Bonny in her
reading.

Abigail Smith married John Adams in 1764

(and from that point on, everyone called her Abigail Adams). They had five children together.

Like John, Abigail was a strong supporter of American independence from Britain—though she knew it would be a long, hard fight. On the night of June 17, 1775, she was awakened at three in the morning by the roar of British guns. Sleep was impossible. At dawn, she took her seven-year-old son, John Quincy, to the top of a hill near their Boston home. And from there, just two miles from the fighting, they watched the bloody Battle of Bunker Hill. The American Revolution would last seven more years.

John Quincy Adams, by the way, was the sixth president of the United States, from 1825 to 1829. Aside from Abigail Adams, Barbara Bush is the only other person to have been both the wife and mother of American presidents.

On March 31, 1776, Abigail wrote her famous "Remember the Ladies" letter to John, who was serving in Congress in Philadelphia. And John really did treat it as a joke. "As to your extraordinary code of laws, I cannot but laugh," he replied. He also threw in the line, "you are so saucy."

Not cool, as Abby told him.

But if John didn't get Abigail's point, lots of other people have. Abigail's letter became a big inspiration to generations of women who followed her.

The details of what a disaster the White House was in November 1800, when Abigail Adams moved in, are all true. "We have not the least fence, yard, or other convenience without," she wrote to her daughter, "and the great unfinished audience room I made a drying room of, to hang up the clothes in."

Another thing Abigail noticed was that much of the work on the building was being done by enslaved African-American men. Abigail spoke strongly against slavery. "It always appeared a most iniquitous [evil] scheme to me," she wrote to John, "to fight ourselves for what we are daily robbing and plundering from those who have as good a right to freedom as we have." Abigail and John agreed that the United States should have banned slavery from the very start. But that would not happen until 1865.

Abigail didn't love being First Lady. She wasn't into fancy parties, and she wasn't one to stand around smiling politely while men discussed important issues. She was smart and funny and had ideas and opinions of her own. John knew this, of course, and relied on her wisdom and advice. Some people thought Abigail had *too* much influence over her husband. They called her "Mrs. President." It was not meant as a compliment. But that didn't stop Abigail

Adams. She paved the way for future First Ladies (and, one day, First Gentlemen) to speak their minds and to work for causes they believe in.

I included the scene where Abigail wrote John a letter (Chapter Ten) because the letters they wrote to each other are so famous. John was away often, serving in Congress or on diplomatic missions in Europe, so the only way they could communicate was by mail. Today you can read more than one thousand of their letters—they're truly a national treasure.

And yes, both Abigail and John began many of their letters to each other with the words, "My dearest friend."

OH NO! NOW FAMOUS FOLKS FROM HISTORY KNOW THEY DON'T HAVE TO DO THE SAME OLD THING ANYMORE—AND EVERYTHING IS TWISTING OUT OF CONTROL!

FIND OUT WHAT HAPPENS IN THE NEXT TIME TWISTERS ADVENTURE.

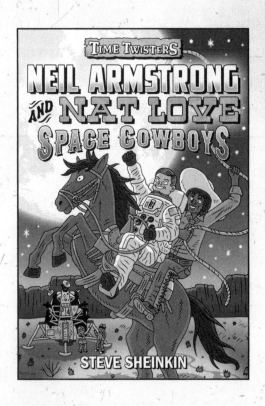

COMING FALL 2018!

CREDITS

STEVE SHEINKIN, *Author*

NEIL SWAAB, *Illustrator / Designer*

CONNIE HSU, *Executive Editor*

SIMON BOUGHTON, *Publisher*

ELIZABETH CLARK, *Art Director*

TOM NAU, *Director of Production*

JILL FRESHNEY, *Senior Executive Managing Editor*

MEGAN ABBATE, *Editorial Assistant*